Sleeping Beauty

retold by VERA SOUTHGATE M A B Com

illustrated by GAVIN ROWE

Ladybird Books

Once upon a time there lived a king and queen who were very happy, except for one thing. They didn't have any children. Every day they said to each other, "If only we had a child!"

Now it happened that, one day, when the queen had been bathing, a frog crept out of the water and spoke to her. It said, "Your wish shall come true. Before a year has gone by, you shall have a daughter."

Every new generation of children is enthralled by the famous stories in our Well Loved Tales series. Younger ones love to have the story read to them. Older children will enjoy the exciting stories in an easy-to-read text.

Revised edition

Published by Ladybird Books Ltd Loughborough Leicestershire UK
Ladybird Books Inc Auburn Maine 04210 USA

Printed in England

The queen was delighted and rushed to
tell her husband the good news.

Within the year, it happened as the frog
had said. A baby daughter was born to
the king and queen. They were both
very happy. The child was lovely and
everyone who came to see her cried,
"What a beautiful baby!"

The king was so proud of his baby
daughter that he ordered a wonderful
christening feast to be prepared.

The king invited all his friends to the feast. He wanted the good fairies to be godmothers to his daughter. There were thirteen fairies in his kingdom, but one was very old and no one had seen her for many years. As the king had only twelve golden plates, he invited just twelve of the fairies. The old fairy was not invited.

When the christening feast was over, the
good fairies went up to the princess, to
give her their magic gifts.

The first fairy said, "You shall have a beautiful face."

The second fairy said, "You shall have kind thoughts."

The third fairy said, "You shall be gentle and loving."

The fourth fairy said, "You shall dance like a leaf in the wind."

The fifth fairy said, "You shall sing like a nightingale."

When eleven of the fairies had given
their gifts, the baby had been promised
everything in the world she could wish
for.

At that moment, the thirteenth fairy suddenly arrived. She was furious because the king had not invited her to the feast. Pointing to the baby, she cried in a loud voice, ''When the king's daughter is fifteen years old, she shall prick her finger on a spindle and fall down dead.''

Without another word she rushed out of the palace.

When they heard the words of the
wicked fairy all the people at the
christening feast gasped in horror. The
queen began to cry and the king didn't
know how to comfort her.

The twelfth fairy, who had not yet given the baby her gift, stepped forward.

"Don't cry," she said. "I shall do what I can to help. I can't undo the evil spell of the wicked fairy, but I can soften it a little."

The twelfth fairy went on, "The
princess will prick her finger on a
spindle, but she will not die. She will
fall into a deep sleep that will last for a
hundred years."

The king thanked the fairy for her kindness. However, he didn't want to think of his daughter sleeping for a hundred years. So he gave orders that every spindle in the kingdom should be burned. Messengers were sent to every town and village to see that this was done.

As time went by, the princess grew into a lovely young girl. All the gifts that the good fairies had promised were hers.

She had a beautiful face. She was thoughtful, gentle and loving. She danced like a leaf in the wind and sang like a nightingale.

The king and queen loved their daughter
very much.

The king and queen were away on the morning of the princess's fifteenth birthday. To amuse herself the princess wandered all over the palace opening doors that she had never seen before.

At last she climbed a narrow winding staircase that led to the top of the highest tower. There she found a little door.

She turned the rusty key in the lock and the door opened. There, in a little room, sat an old woman at her spinning wheel busily spinning flax.

"Good day," said the princess. "What are you doing?"

"I am spinning, my child," replied the old woman.

"Oh, how wonderful!" cried the princess. "Please let me try."

No sooner had the princess touched the spindle than the words of the wicked fairy came true. She pricked her finger.

As soon as she felt the prick of the
spindle, the princess fell upon the bed,
in a deep sleep.

The old woman fell asleep upon her
chair. Every other living creature in the
palace also fell asleep.

At that very moment, the king and
queen returned home for their
daughter's birthday. They fell asleep in
the great hall of the palace. The lords
and ladies who were with them fell
asleep nearby.

In the stables, the horses slept. The dogs in the courtyard, the pigeons on the roof and the flies on the wall all fell asleep.

In the kitchen, the fire died out and the meat stopped cooking. The cook had been just about to box the scullery boy's ears, because of something he had forgotten to do. But the cook fell asleep and so did the scullery boy.

The whole palace became silent. The wind dropped and not a leaf stirred on the trees in the palace garden.

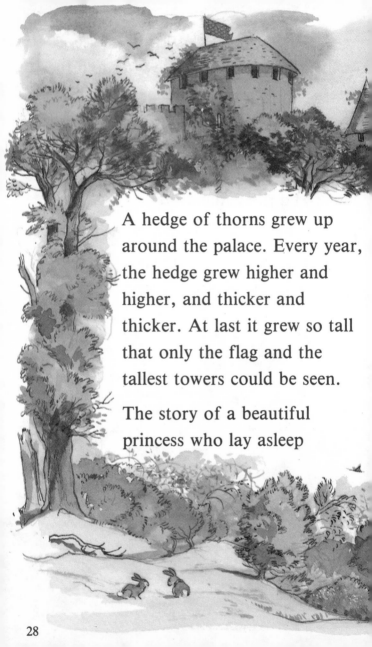

A hedge of thorns grew up around the palace. Every year, the hedge grew higher and higher, and thicker and thicker. At last it grew so tall that only the flag and the tallest towers could be seen.

The story of a beautiful princess who lay asleep

spread throughout the
kingdom and far beyond.
She became known as
Sleeping Beauty.

Many princes travelled to the
palace, hoping to wake her.
But the thorn hedge grew so
thickly that no one could
force their way through.

Many years later, a prince from another land visited the kingdom of Sleeping Beauty. An old man told him a tale which he had heard from his grandfather.

The tale was of a palace, hidden behind a thick hedge of thorns. Inside, a beautiful princess, known as Sleeping Beauty, lay asleep. It was said that everyone in the palace had been asleep for a hundred years.

When the prince heard the old man's story, he said, "I must see this beautiful princess and try to wake her."

"Ah! But wait," cried the old man. "It is too dangerous. I have heard that, through the years, many princes have tried to break through the hedge. No one could do it."

"I'm not afraid," replied the prince. "I must try to see this lovely princess."

Now it happened that the very day on which the prince arrived was exactly a hundred years after Sleeping Beauty had fallen asleep. The evil spell of the wicked fairy had come to its end.

As the prince began to push against the
hedge of thorns, every thorn turned into
a lovely rose. The hedge opened to let
him pass through.

At last he came to the courtyard of the palace, where the dogs lay sleeping. On the roof the pigeons sat asleep. In the stables he found the horses, all standing asleep.

Not a sound was to be heard in the whole of the palace.

Next the prince went into the kitchen.
He saw the flies asleep on the wall. The
fire was out and the meat was half
cooked.

The cook stood asleep, with his arms stretched out towards the scullery boy. The scullery boy had fallen asleep, just as he was running away from the cook.

At last the prince came to the foot of
the highest tower. He began to climb the
narrow, winding staircase. When he
reached the door at the top, he pushed it
open and stepped into the small room.

There, on the bed, the most beautiful
girl he had ever seen lay asleep. The
prince could not take his eyes from her
face.

He looked at her for a long time, then
he bent over and kissed her.

At that moment Sleeping Beauty opened her eyes and gave the prince a wonderful smile. The prince took her hand and she stood up. Together they went down into the great hall.

The whole palace had begun to stir. In the great hall the king and queen and their lords and ladies woke up.

In the kitchen the fire began to burn and the meat began to cook. The scullery boy ran off before the cook could box his ears.

The dogs in the courtyard began to bark. In the stables the horses stirred. The pigeons on the roof flew away. The palace had come to life after a hundred years.

A wonderful wedding feast was prepared. Sleeping Beauty and the prince were married and they lived happily ever after.